First encyclopedia

TWO CAN

Copyright © 2005 Two-Can Publishing

Two-Can Publishing
An imprint of Creative Publishing international, Inc.
18705 Lake Drive East
Chanhassen, MN 55317
1-800-328-3895
www.two-canpublishing.com

Created by Bookwork Limited
Unit 17, Piccadilly Mill, Lower Street, Stroud,
Gloucestershire, GL5 2HT

Literacy consultant: Nicola Morgan

ISBN 1-58728-440-5

Library of Congress Cataloging-in-Publication Data

Taylor, Barbara, date.
  Two-Can first encyclopedia: the essential first reference book for young
readers / Barbara Taylor.
    p. cm.
  ISBN 1-58728-440-5
  1. Children's encyclopedias and dictionaries. I. Two-Can (Firm) II. Title.
  AG6.T39 2005
  031—dc22
                                                    2004014461

        1 2 3 4 5 6 09 08 07 06 05 04

Printed in Malaysia

First

TWO CAN

encyclopedia

Barbara Taylor

Contents

All About You

People and Places

Plants and Animals

The Natural World

On the Move

Everyday Things

Your Body

Inside your body is a bony skeleton that gives the body its shape and protects organs such as the heart, lungs, and brain. Muscles around the bones allow you to move. Your skin holds all your parts together.

Fingerprints

The skin on the tips of your fingers has swirly patterns in it. If you dip a fingertip in paint or ink and press it onto paper, it makes a mark called a fingerprint. Each person's fingerprints are different.

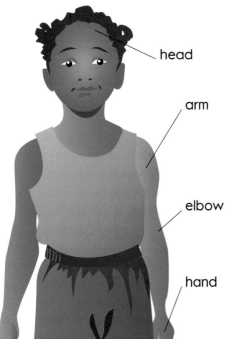

head

arm

elbow

hand

knee

leg

foot

Senses

You have five main senses: sight, hearing, smell, taste, and touch. Your sense of touch is all over your body, in your skin. The other senses work through sense organs on your head. These sense organs are your eyes, ears, nose, and tongue.

This part of your ear collects sounds from the air. Your brain figures out what the sounds mean.

Skin lets you feel everything it touches.

Body parts

Look at the picture to see the names of some of the different parts of the human body. Can you find the parts on your own body?

Mouth and teeth

Your mouth is like a door that opens to let food into your body. Your hard, strong teeth bite and chew your food into small pieces that you can swallow. Don't forget to brush your teeth after meals and at bedtime to keep them clean and strong!

Your flat back teeth crush and grind food.

Your sharp front teeth bite and tear food.

Your eyes send pictures of the world to your brain.

Your nose can sense thousands of different smells.

Your tongue senses sweet, sour, salty, and bitter tastes.

Find out more
Growing Up – page 8
What People Eat – page 16
Light and Color – page 56
Sounds and Music – page 58

Health

Your body needs a variety of healthy foods and plenty of water to keep it working well. It also needs sleep and exercise. You exercise your body by being active. Running, swimming, dancing, and other sports are good forms of exercise.

Growing Up

Find out more
Your Body – page 6
Special Days – page 10
Jobs People Do – page 14

You started life as a tiny baby. Your parents had to feed you, dress you, and do everything for you. Now you are a child and can do lots of things for yourself. Next, you will grow into a teenager, and then into an adult. Even adults change as they get older.

Baby

Babies grow very fast during the first few months of their lives. By the time they are one year old, most babies can sit up, crawl, and stand up. Some can even walk! They also try to say their first words.

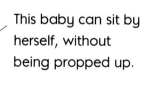

This baby can sit by herself, without being propped up.

Child

As a baby grows taller, heavier, and stronger, we begin to think of him or her as a child. At around six years old, a child's first set of teeth begins to fall out. Adult teeth grow in their place.

Adult

As a person reaches the end of the teenage years, he or she stops growing. This person is an adult. Some adults become parents and have children of their own. Children usually look like their parents or other members of their family. But everyone is different. There is no one else quite like you—unless you have an identical twin!

Older people have had more life experiences, so they can share what they have learned with younger people.

Old age

As adults become older, their bodies change. Their muscles become weaker, their skin wrinkles, and their hair turns gray or white. Their senses of sight, hearing, and taste may not work as well. Some people live to be grandparents or even great-grandparents!

Special Days

Some of the days in your life are very special. These days may be family celebrations, national holidays, or dates that are important to your religion. On special days, people may dress up, give presents, sing songs, or share good meals.

Weddings

A wedding is a ceremony that takes place when two people get married. The bride and groom agree to spend their lives together. They promise to love and care for each other. Some weddings are religious ceremonies, while others are not.

Find out more

Growing Up – page 8
What People Eat – page 16
Clothes People Wear – page 18

National holidays

Certain days, such as New Year's Day and May Day, are holidays in many countries. In the United States, Thanksgiving is a holiday in November. People give thanks for the good things they have. Families often eat a special meal of turkey and pumpkin pie.

Hindu brides wear red because it is a bright, happy color.

Hindu bride and groom in India

10

A Hindu groom often wears a special hat called a tupi, or a turban made to look like a crown.

Your family and friends wrap presents to give you on your birthday.

The number of candles on your birthday cake show how old you are.

Birthdays

You celebrate the day you were born on your birthday. You may have a party with your family and friends. A birthday happens once a year. When is your next birthday? How old will you be?

Religious festivals

People around the world follow different religions. Each one has its own festivals. Easter and Christmas are two important days for Christians. Jews celebrate Hannukah, a festival of lights, in winter. Id-ul-Fitr is a Muslim festival that happens at the end of the holy month of Ramadan. For Hindus, Divali is a time to celebrate the goodness in the world. Festivals in the Buddhist faith often include giving gifts of food to the poor.

Where People Live

The place where you live is your home. Your home keeps you warm, dry, and safe. It is where you sleep and spend time with your family. Homes come in all shapes and sizes, from apartments and houses to tents and caravans.

Towns and cities

Nearly half of the people in the world live in towns and cities. A town or city is a group of homes, stores, and other buildings that are built near each other. A city is bigger than a town, and it often has more noise and traffic.

Apartment buildings

In big cities, there is not much space for homes. Some people live close together in tall buildings called apartment buildings. One of these buildings can hold homes for many people.

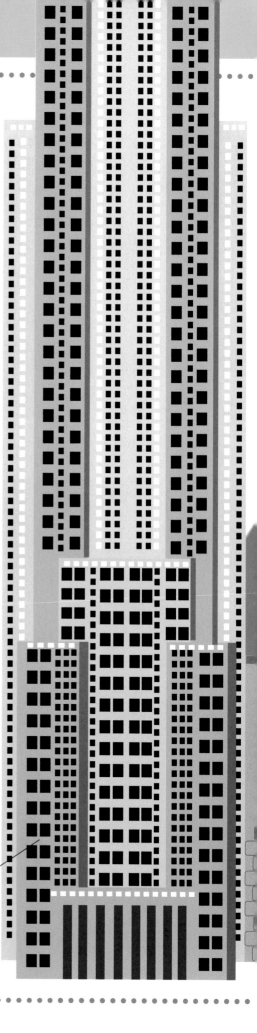

These apartment buildings are made of concrete, steel, and glass.

Find out more
The Weather – page 42
Rocks and Soil – page 44
What Things Are Made Of – page 54

Bedouin tent

Building materials

Homes are built out of all kinds of materials, such as wood from trees, and stone or clay dug out of the ground. Clay can be baked into bricks. Sand is made into glass for windows. Concrete and steel are made in factories.

Movable homes

Homes such as tents and mobile homes can be moved from place to place. Some people do this because they need to go wherever they can find food and water for their animals. Other people simply do not want to stay in one place.

Bricks are hard and strong. They can be made in different shapes, sizes, and colors.

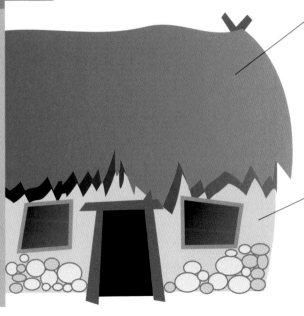

This home's grass roof helps to hold in heat.

Stone walls last a long time and keep out the cold and rain.

Jobs People Do

What would you like to be when you grow up? Would you like to have a job helping people, or playing sports? Perhaps you would like to grow things or make things. In many jobs, people work together as a team.

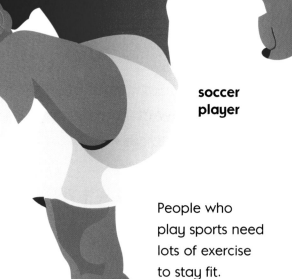

soccer player

People who play sports need lots of exercise to stay fit.

Makers

Many jobs involve making things. Chefs make food, construction workers make buildings, and weavers make rugs. In factories, workers make goods such as toys, cars, clothing, and paper.

painter's tools

Sports

A few very skilled people can make a living playing a sport, such as tennis, soccer, or baseball. Other sports jobs include training or coaching players and covering sports news on television or radio.

Helpers

If you like to help people, you could be a doctor, a nurse, or an ambulance driver. You could be a teacher. Or you work as a police officer or a firefighter and keep people safe.

Entertainers

From clowns and actors to singers, musicians, and dancers, entertainers help us to enjoy our spare time. These people have to spend a lot of time practicing their skills.

Farmers

Farmers work on the land to produce food for us to eat. They sow crops, such as wheat and rice. They also raise animals, such as chickens, cattle, sheep, pigs, and goats.

Some farmers use powerful tractors to pull heavy machines such as plows.

Find out more

Where People Live – page 12
Clothes People Wear – page 18
Rocks and Soil – page 44
Traveling on Land – page 50

farmer driving a tractor

What People Eat

You need food to stay alive. It's best to eat lots of different foods, especially healthy ones like fruits, vegetables, milk products, meat, and fish. This is called a balanced diet. But many people in the world struggle just to have enough food to survive.

Fruit and vegetables

You should eat at least five kinds of vegetables and fruit every day. They are full of vitamins and fiber, which help to keep you healthy.

Lemons and limes contain vitamin C.

cheese and vegetable pizza

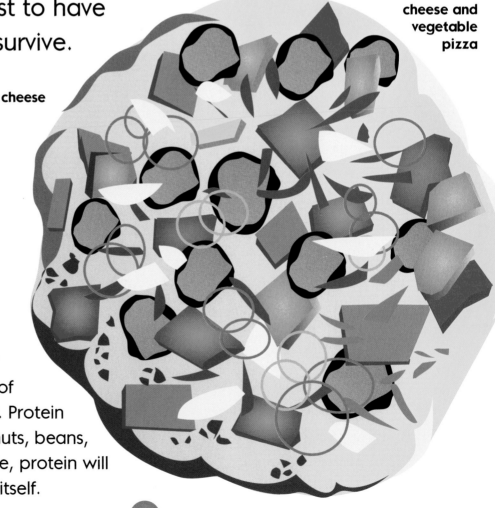

cheese

Food for growth

Until you are about twenty years old, your body will need plenty of protein to help it grow. Protein is found in meat, fish, nuts, beans, and cheese. Later in life, protein will help your body repair itself.

You get most of your energy from carbohydrates, such as rice, pasta, bread, potatoes, and cereal.

bowl of rice

Food for energy

The energy that food contains is set free inside your body so you can use it for moving around, staying warm, and keeping your body working. You also use energy for talking, thinking, reading, and sleeping.

Choose fruit juices or fruit-flavored drinks that do not contain too much sugar. Sugary foods are not good for your weight or for your teeth.

Preserving food

Foods such as vegetables, fruit, meats, and coffee can be dried, frozen, or pickled, then sealed in jars, cans, or other air-tight packages. This keeps it safe to eat for a long time. But fresh foods are usually better for you.

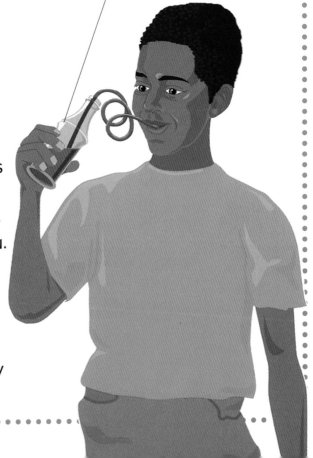

Water

Your body needs lots of water. Make sure you drink plenty of water every day. Did you know that about two-thirds of your body is water?

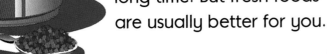

Clothes People Wear

Clothes cover and protect your body. They keep you warm when it is cold, and keep you dry when it is raining. Grown-ups often wear special clothes, such as uniforms, to do their jobs. But everyone gets dressed up in special clothes for parties or celebrations.

Special clothes

Some people, such as nurses, wear uniforms so you can recognize them. You may wear a school uniform. People sometimes have to wear special clothes for protection. Wetsuits keep divers dry and warm underwater. Spacesuits protect astronauts against the sun's rays and give them air to breathe.

What clothes are made of

Some clothes are made of natural materials, which come from plants and animals. Other clothes are made of artificial materials, which are made in factories.

sheep

Wool is a natural material. People cut the wool from sheep, and it grows back again.

wool yarn

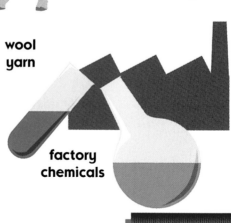

Polyester and nylon are artificial materials made from chemicals.

factory chemicals

nylon thread

Find out more

man living in North Africa

Hot and cold

In hot places, people often wear loose, light clothes made of cotton or other natural materials. In cold places, people wear layers of clothes made of wool, fur, or fluffy fibers, which trap body heat and keep them warm.

This man's clothes help to protect him from the heat of the sun.

speedskater

This speedskater's outfit is made of stretchy fabric and hugs her body tightly.

Sports

Clothes for dancing and playing sports must be comfortable so people can move easily. Dancers, gymnasts, and skaters usually wear close-fitting costumes.

Boots support the skater's ankles.

Plants and Fungi

Plants are living things that use light, water, and air to make food in their leaves. Fungi are not plants, because they cannot make their own food. Most plants—even trees—have flowers. Other plants, such as ferns and mosses, do not have flowers.

Plant parts

Most plants are made up of four different parts. The roots grow underground. The stem holds up the plant. The leaves are usually thin, flat, and green. Their job is to make sugary food for the plant. The flowers are often colorful. They make seeds, which grow into new plants.

Mosses and ferns

Some plants, such as mosses and ferns, do not have flowers and cannot make seeds. Instead, they make small, simple plant parts called spores. Spores grow into new plants. They can survive long dry spells or other bad weather.

the sun

The sun's energy

Plants use the green color in their leaves to soak up the sun's energy. They use this energy to make food. Animals cannot make their own food. They must eat to stay alive.

The strong stem holds the flower and leaves up above the soil.

The veins inside the leaves are thin pipes that carry food and water.

Roots hold the plant firmly in the soil and soak up water.

Flowers often have colorful petals and a lovely smell to attract insects. Insects help the plant make seeds.

Fungi

Fungi don't have roots, stems, leaves, or flowers. Most of the time, they are just a clump of threads in the soil. The threads join together, then push their way above the ground. Mushrooms are a common fungus.

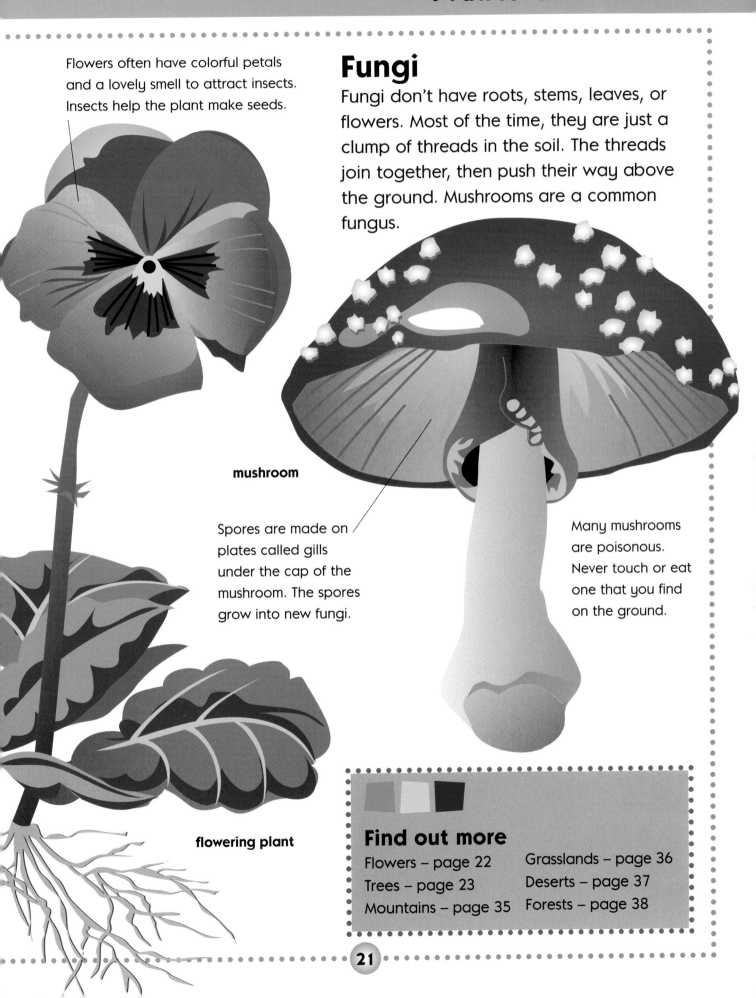

mushroom

Spores are made on plates called gills under the cap of the mushroom. The spores grow into new fungi.

Many mushrooms are poisonous. Never touch or eat one that you find on the ground.

flowering plant

Find out more

Flowers – page 22

Trees – page 23

Mountains – page 35

Grasslands – page 36

Deserts – page 37

Forests – page 38

Flowers

The job of a flower is to bring pollen and eggs together to make new plants. The young plants are protected inside tough seeds, which contain food. The plants use this food when they begin to grow.

Pollen

The male parts of a flower make a yellow dust called pollen. This may join with the eggs in the same flower or another flower of the same kind. Wind, water, insects, and other animals spread pollen from flower to flower.

Spreading seeds

Seeds are spread away from their parent plants by wind, rain, or animals. If they land on good soil and have light, air, and water, they will start to grow.

dandelion seeds ready to blow away

Pollen need to land on top of this platform, called the stigma.

Pollen is made in sacs on stalks called stamens.

Pollen moves from the stigma down a stalk called the style to reach the eggs in the middle of the flower.

Colorful petals attract insects, which carry pollen from flower to flower.

Eggs are in a case, where they develop into seeds.

Trees

Trees are large plants that have a woody trunk. Some trees live for thousands of years. Evergreen trees, such as pines, keep their leaves all year round. Deciduous trees, such as oaks, drop their leaves in autumn and grow new ones in spring.

crown

A tree has three main parts: the crown, the trunk, and the roots.

trunk

oak tree

roots

A tree grows a new ring in its trunk every year. Count the rings on this tree stump to figure out how old this tree was when it was cut down.

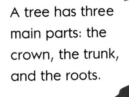

Tree leaves

Some trees, such as oaks and maples, have wide, flat leaves. Other trees, such as pines and firs, have thin, narrow, waxy leaves that look like needles. Needles keep the tree from losing too much water in the winter.

Uses for wood

People cut down trees and use the wood to make lots of things, from toys and paper to houses and furniture. New trees can be planted to replace those that are cut down.

Insects

There are over a million kinds of insects in the world. All insects have six legs and three body parts. Their skeleton is on the outside of their body. Most insects have wings and can fly. They have two feelers, called antennae, on their head.

Life cycle

Most insects hatch out of eggs. Many of them look different from their parents. These insects eat and grow until they are ready to change into adults. Other insects look like small adults when they hatch.

wing

The wasp has a stinger under its back end to help protect itself from enemies.

The front part of the body is called the head.

eye

The back part of the body is the abdomen.

Senses

Insects have eyes, but no tongue or nose. They use their antennae to feel and smell. They taste with many parts of the body—even their feet!

antenna

The middle part of the body is the thorax.

Tiny hairs on a wasp's body pick up sounds from the air.

leg

wasp

Invertebrates

Insects are part of a larger group of creatures called invertebrates. Invertebrates have one thing in common: They do not have a skeleton inside their bodies. Some have a hard skin or shell for protection. Others are soft and squishy.

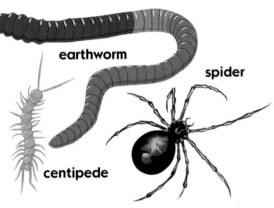

earthworm

spider

centipede

A snail's eyes are on the ends of these long tentacles.

How many legs?

Different invertebrates have different numbers of legs. Spiders have eight legs. Centipedes have about thirty legs. Earthworms don't have any.

Find out more
Amphibians – page 27
Reptiles – page 28
Rocks and Soil – page 44

snail

A snail carries its home around on its back!

Snails

A snail slides along on one wide, slimy foot. On its back, a snail has a hard shell that grows in a spiral shape. The snail can pull its body inside its shell to hide from enemies.

Fish

Thousands of different kinds of fish live in oceans, lakes, and rivers. They breathe through gills and have a skeleton inside their body. Most fish have a bony skeleton, but sharks and rays have a skeleton made of rubbery material called cartilage.

A ray flaps its large side fins like wings to "fly" through the water.

ray

An eel is a very long, thin fish. It wriggles its whole body to move in the water.

eel

goldfish

tail

Most fish sweep their tail fin from side to side to push themselves forward. Their other fins steer and keep their body steady.

fin

Most fish are covered in scales.

The gills are under this cover.

Find out more
Oceans, Lakes, and Rivers – page 40
Ice, Water, and Steam – page 55

Breathing

To breathe, fish gulp a big mouthful of water. They force the water to flow over thin flaps of skin called gills before it flows out of their body again. The gills take air from the water and send it into the fish's blood.

Amphibians

Amphibians include frogs, toads, and salamanders. Most of them lay eggs in water. These eggs hatch into tadpoles, which breathe through gills. Most adult amphibians breathe through lungs as well as through their wet skin.

Newts and salamanders

These amphibians have a long tail. They eat creatures such as slugs and worms. Many newts and salamanders have poisonous skin. Their bright colors warn enemies to stay away.

salamander

Frogs and toads

Adult frogs and toads have a big, wide mouth for swallowing food such as insects and worms. They do not have a tail. Most frogs have long back legs and are good at jumping.

Large eyes spot food and danger.

eardrum

Many frogs have a throat pouch, which makes their calls louder.

treefrog

Treefrogs have sticky toes to cling to trees.

Reptiles

Reptiles have a scaly body with a bony skeleton inside. Most of them live on land, especially in warm places. Baby reptiles usually hatch out of eggs. There are many kinds of reptiles, including turtles, tortoises, lizards, snakes, crocodiles, and alligators.

Lizards

Most lizards are quick-moving hunters of insects and other small creatures. They usually have four legs, sharp claws, and long tails. Chameleons, geckos, and iguanas are all types of lizards.

Crocodiles

Crocodiles are the biggest of all reptiles. They are fierce hunters with huge jaws full of sharp teeth. They eat insects, frogs, fish, birds, and even large mammals, such as zebras.

1

3

2

4

crocodile

Eyes and nose holes are on the top of the head.

Baby turtles

A female sea turtle lays her eggs on a beach (1). She digs a hole for her eggs (2) and then covers them with sand. When the baby turtles hatch (3), they race to the sea (4), where they will live and grow.

Find out more

Insects – page 24
Invertebrates – page 25
Birds – page 30

Deserts – page 37
Oceans, Lakes, and
Rivers – page 40

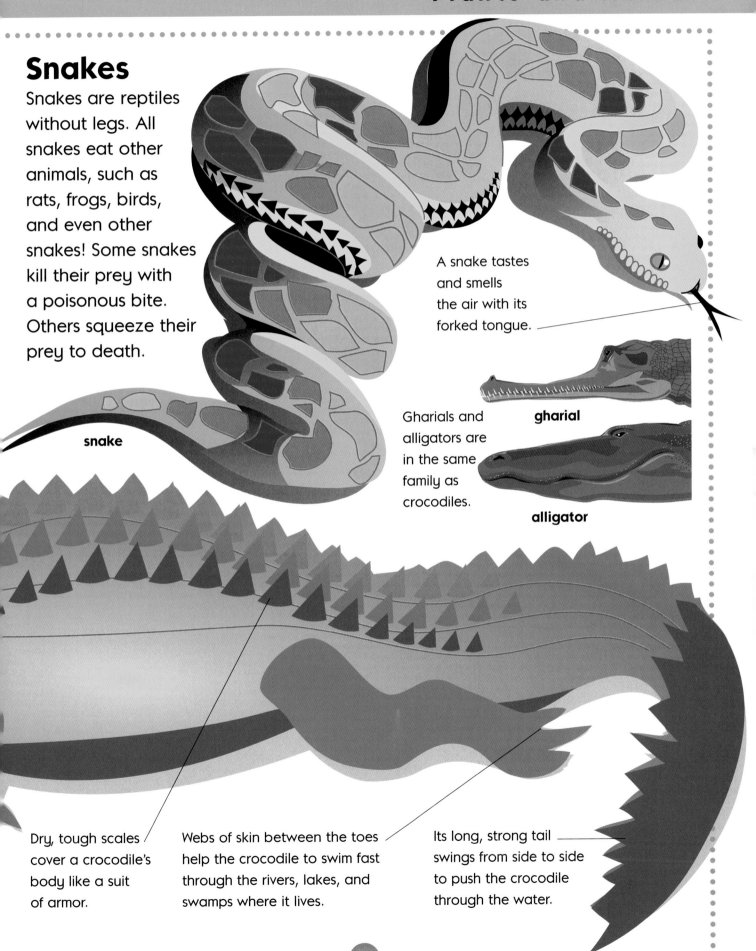

Snakes

Snakes are reptiles without legs. All snakes eat other animals, such as rats, frogs, birds, and even other snakes! Some snakes kill their prey with a poisonous bite. Others squeeze their prey to death.

snake

A snake tastes and smells the air with its forked tongue.

Gharials and alligators are in the same family as crocodiles.

gharial

alligator

Dry, tough scales cover a crocodile's body like a suit of armor.

Webs of skin between the toes help the crocodile to swim fast through the rivers, lakes, and swamps where it lives.

Its long, strong tail swings from side to side to push the crocodile through the water.

Birds

Birds are the only animals with feathers. They have two wings instead of arms. Most birds use their wings to fly. Inside their bodies, birds have a bony skeleton and lungs for breathing air. Birds live in many different habitats around the world.

Eggs

All birds lay eggs with a hard eggshell. Most birds build nests to keep their eggs and babies safe. Parents sit on their eggs to keep them warm until they are ready to hatch.

pigeon egg

ostrich egg

Compared to a pigeon's egg, an ostrich's egg is very large.

baby duck

Find out more

Baby birds

Some baby birds are born with feathers. They can see and run around soon after they hatch from the egg. Other baby birds are naked, blind, and helpless when they hatch.

woodpecker

eye

bill

Flying

The shape of a bird's wings and feathers depends a lot on how it finds food. Eagles' large wings allow it to fly quietly as it hunts. A hummingbird's wings move quickly so it can hang in the air to drink from a flower.

Birds flap their wings up and down to fly through the air.

Birds have scaly legs and feet. They have three or four toes that are tipped with sharp, curved claws.

tail

Bills

Birds use their bills to catch and eat their food. A spoonbill sweeps its bill from side to side through the water to catch food. A pelican's bill is good for scooping up fish. Eagles use their hooked bills to tear apart mice and other prey.

spoonbill

pelican

eagle

Mammals

You are a mammal. A mammal is a kind of animal with fur or hair to keep it warm. A baby mammal feeds on its mother's milk. Mammals breathe air and keep their bodies at the same warm temperature all the time. They are smart creatures.

Find out more
Cold Lands – page 34
Grasslands – page 36
Deserts – page 37
Forests – page 38

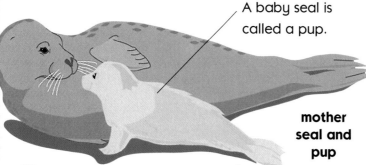

A baby seal is called a pup.

mother seal and pup

A baby kangaroo is called a joey. It spends its first six to nine months living inside its mother's pouch.

Ocean mammals

A few mammals live in the ocean. Dolphins, whales, manatees, sea cows, and dugongs give birth to their babies in the water. They never leave the water. Seals, sea lions, and walruses spend time in the ocean, but they give birth on land.

Baby pouches

Some mammal babies finish growing in a pouch on their mother's belly. They drink their mother's milk while they are inside the pouch.

mother kangaroo and joey

A mother lion may carry her small cubs in her mouth. This does not hurt them.

Growing up

Mammal parents such as this lioness take care of their babies until they are old enough to survive on their own. The adults protect their young and teach them to find food.

Pets

Many of the pets people keep in their homes are mammals. Large mammal pets include dogs and cats. Small mammal pets include mice, rats, hamsters, gerbils, guinea pigs, and rabbits.

A baby lion is called a cub.

Lions are just one kind of mammal. There are more than 4,000 different kinds of mammals in the world.

lioness and cub

Cold Lands

At the top and bottom of the world are cold, windy lands covered with ice and snow. Many animals visit these lands only in the summer, when the weather is warmer and there is plenty to eat.

Find out more
Birds – page 30
Mammals – page 32
Oceans, Lakes, and Rivers
– page 40
Ice, Water, and Steam
– page 55

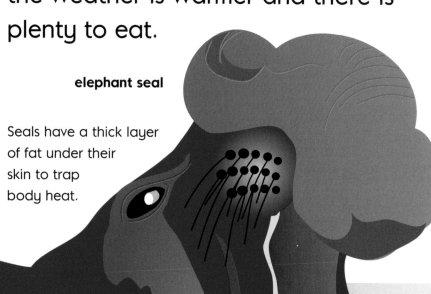

elephant seal

Seals have a thick layer of fat under their skin to trap body heat.

Penguins

Many kinds of penguins live in cold oceans in the bottom half of the world. They use their stiff, narrow wings for swimming underwater. Penguins cannot fly.

king penguins

Keeping warm

In cold lands, animals keep warm with a thick fur coat, a layer of fat, or feathers. The Arctic fox curls its thick, furry tail around its body to keep out the cold.

Mountains

The tops of mountains are cold and windy, and the rocky slopes are steep and slippery. Plants grow close to the ground to keep out of the freezing wind. Many of them have thick, hairy leaves that trap heat and moisture.

Birds

The air high in the mountains does not contain much oxygen, which many animals need to breathe to stay alive. Birds have good lungs that help them to breathe mountain air. Many birds, such as condors, can fly well in strong winds.

Made for mountain living

Llamas have hooves that grip well as they leap up steep slopes. Like many mountain mammals, they have thick fur to keep them warm. Some small animals go into a deep sleep called hibernation during the coldest months. Birds have feathers for protection.

Chinchillas do not hibernate. They grow a long, thick fur coat in winter. Their summer coat is made of shorter, thinner fur.

mother chinchilla and young

Grasslands

Find out more
Plants and Fungi
– page 20
Insects – page 24
Birds – page 30
Mammals – page 32

Grasslands grow where the weather is too dry and the soil is too poor for most trees to grow. Many animals eat the grass. Small animals burrow underneath the grass to escape from enemies or other dangers. On hot grasslands, tiny insects called termites build towers of mud in which to live.

Ostriches live in the grasslands of Africa. They cannot fly, but they run very fast.

zebra and foal

ostrich

A baby zebra is called a foal. It can run when it is only a few hours old.

Birds

Some grassland birds, such as ostriches, feed on grass seeds and insects. Others, such as vultures, feed on dead animals. With vultures around, no food is wasted.

Mammals

Grassland mammals include plant eaters such as zebras, elephants, giraffes, rabbits, kangaroos, and wild horses. Many of them live in large groups so that they have help spotting danger. Meat eaters such as foxes, lions, and hyenas hunt the plant eaters.

Deserts

Deserts are sandy or rocky places where it hardly ever rains. It is usually very hot during the day and freezing cold at night. Desert plants and animals have to be tough. Some animals hide in burrows during the day and come out at night when it is cool.

Plants

Some desert plants, such as cactuses, store water in their stems or leaves. They have both long, deep roots and lots of shallow roots, just under the surface, to collect as much water as possible.

cactus

Camels have two rows of long eyelashes to keep sand out of their eyes.

Elf owls live in holes in cactuses.

Reptiles

Many snakes, lizards, tortoises, and other reptiles live in deserts. They have watertight skin to hold in moisture, and they can live a long time without food and water.

camel

Mammals

Camels survive well in the desert. They store fat in their humps. They can break down this fat to produce food and water when they cannot find enough to eat and drink.

37

Forests

Forests are places where lots of trees cover the land. Many animals live in forests because the trees there provide food and shelter. The main types of forests are warm deciduous forests, hot rain forests, and cool coniferous forests.

Winter survival

Some forest mammals grow thick fur coats in winter. Others, such as dormice, go into a deep sleep called hibernation. Some birds fly away from the forest in autumn and return in spring.

Find out more

Deciduous forests

Deciduous is the name for trees that lose their leaves in cold or dry seasons. Deciduous forests have warm summers and cool winters.

A baby deer, or fawn, has spots that make it harder to see in the shady forest. Coloring that helps an animal hide is called camouflage.

baby deer

Deer have long legs to help them run away fast from danger.

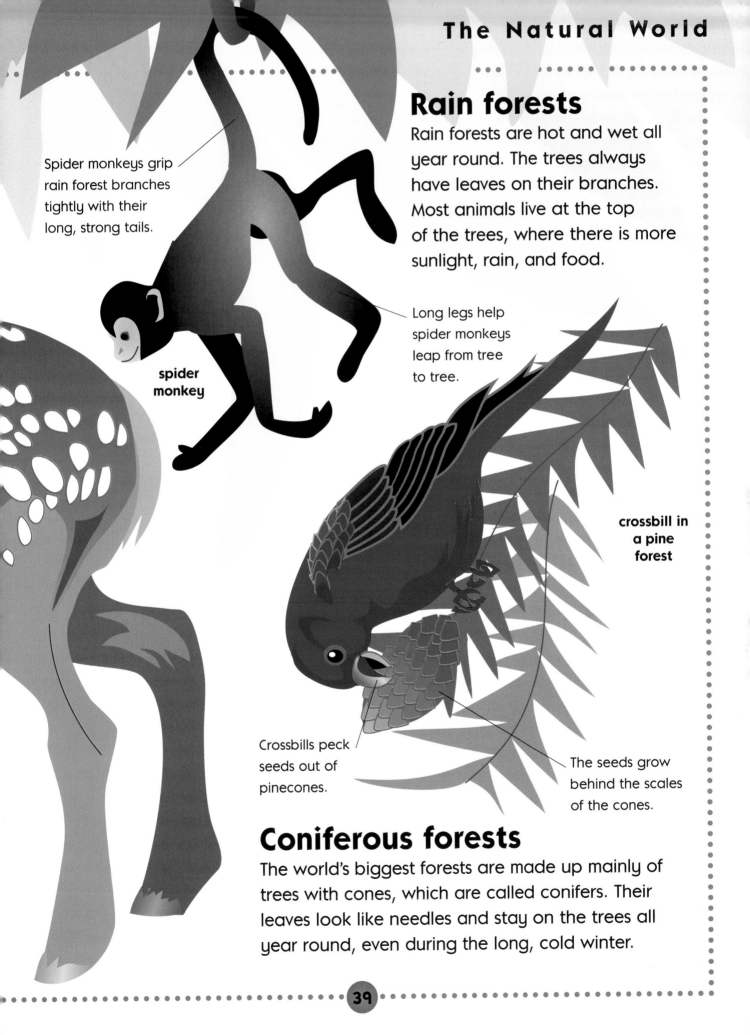

Spider monkeys grip rain forest branches tightly with their long, strong tails.

spider monkey

Rain forests

Rain forests are hot and wet all year round. The trees always have leaves on their branches. Most animals live at the top of the trees, where there is more sunlight, rain, and food.

Long legs help spider monkeys leap from tree to tree.

crossbill in a pine forest

Crossbills peck seeds out of pinecones.

The seeds grow behind the scales of the cones.

Coniferous forests

The world's biggest forests are made up mainly of trees with cones, which are called conifers. Their leaves look like needles and stay on the trees all year round, even during the long, cold winter.

Oceans, Lakes, and Rivers

More than half of the world is covered in salty ocean water. On land, rainwater collects in rivers, lakes, and ponds. This water is called freshwater because it is not salty. Both freshwater and saltwater are full of life.

Hippopotamuses live in lakes and rivers in Africa.

Ocean life

All life in the oceans depends on tiny plants and animals called plankton, which float on top of the water. Many ocean animals, from shrimps to whales, eat this plankton.

Hippos' skin makes an oily pink sunscreen that keeps them from getting a sunburn.

Octopuses swim by pumping out a jet of water, which makes them shoot backward.

The ocean floor

Deep down in the oceans, it is dark and very cold. Many fish glow in the dark to attract a meal or surprise enemies. Animals called sponges are attached to the sea floor, while worms burrow in the mud.

Octopuses have eight arms called tentacles.

Angelfish live on coral reefs.

Coral reefs

Corals are tiny animals that grow in warm, shallow oceans. The corals grow on top of each other to form a raised area called a reef. A reef is home to a huge variety of animals, from octopuses and fish to crabs and sea slugs.

When a hippo opens its huge mouth, it means "Watch out! I'm dangerous!"

Find out more
Fish – page 26
Reptiles – page 28
Mammals – page 32

Hippos can stay under the water for more than 15 minutes.

Lakes and rivers

Animals that live in lakes and rivers are good swimmers. River dolphins have a powerful tail to push them through the water. Otters and beavers have webbed feet to help them swim.

The Weather

tornado

Weather happens because air warms up and cools down. Warm air rises in the sky and then cools down to make clouds and rain. Cool air moves in to fill the space left by the warm, rising air. This moving air makes wind.

Seasons

In most parts of the world, the weather changes in a similar way every year to give four seasons, which are called spring, summer, autumn, and winter. Some hot places have only two seasons, called the wet season and the dry season.

Storms

Storms are times of bad weather, when strong winds blow and heavy rain or snow falls. They happen when big areas of warm and cold air crash together, or when there is a lot of heat and water in the air.

A tornado is a spinning cloud. The winds in a tornado spin at hundreds of miles an hour and can damage homes and trees.

A tornado sucks up things, just like a vacuum cleaner.

Clouds and rain

Clouds are made of drops of water hanging in the sky. When the drops become too heavy to stay up in the air, they fall to the ground as rain. If the sun shines when it is raining, you may see a rainbow!

Umbrellas, boots, and raincoats keep you dry in wet weather.

snowflakes

Find out more

Snow and ice

Snow is rain that gets very cold and freezes as it falls from clouds. Each snowflake shape has six points but every snowflake has a different pattern. When the weather gets warmer, the snow melts back into water again.

Rocks and Soil

The Earth is made of rocks with layers of soil on top. Plants grow in the soil, and some animals make their homes there. Far underground, in the middle of Earth, it is very hot. Rocks there are not hard. They are melted into a liquid.

Gems are cut and polished to make jewels.

Metals and gems

Some rocks contain metals such as iron, copper, gold, or silver. Some rocks contain beautiful gems such as diamonds or opals. Most gems are formed by heat or pressure on rocks that are deep underground.

Soil

Rain and ice break up rocks into little pieces, which build up to make soil. Soil also contains the remains of dead plants and animals. These add good things to the soil and help plants to grow.

mole digging a burrow

Moles dig tunnels in the soil with their strong front paws.

Life in the soil

Millions of small animals, such as worms and ants, live in the soil. Some underground animals, such as moles, are much bigger. When animals dig burrows, they mix up the soil and make space for air and water to move through the soil.

Volcanoes

Melted rock from inside Earth sometimes pushes its way to the surface. It bursts out of openings called volcanoes. The hot rock, called lava, turns hard as it cools. Layers of cooled lava pile up to make mountains shaped like cones.

Find out more
Plants and Fungi – page 20
Invertebrates – page 25
The Solar System – page 46
What Things Are Made Of – page 54

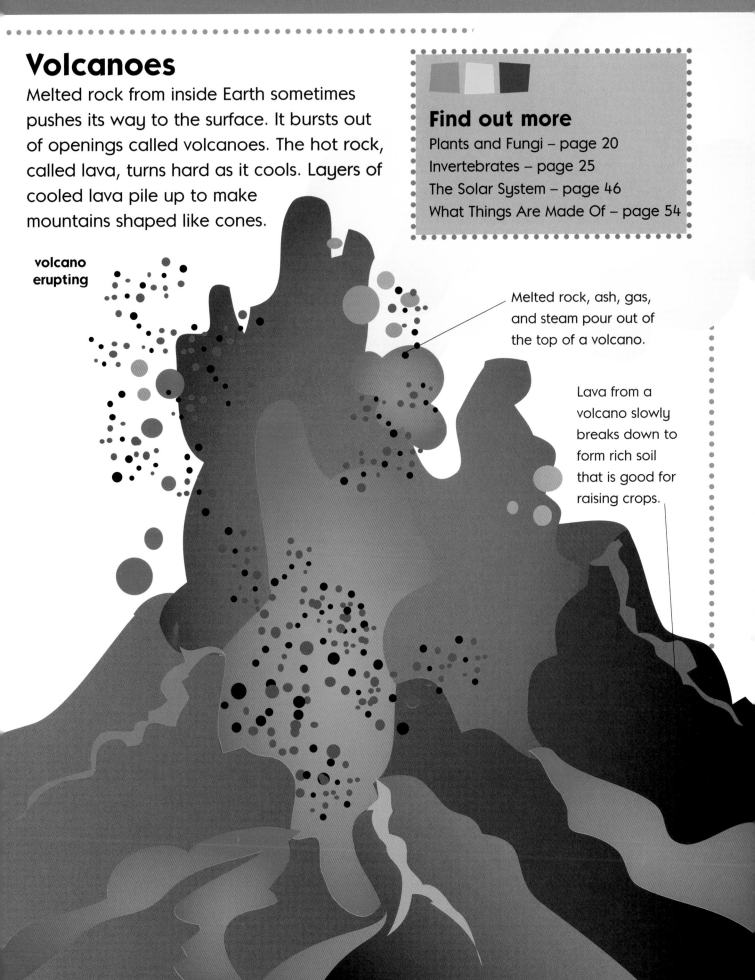

volcano
erupting

Melted rock, ash, gas, and steam pour out of the top of a volcano.

Lava from a volcano slowly breaks down to form rich soil that is good for raising crops.

The Solar System

We live on a huge ball of rock called Earth. Earth is a planet that circles around a star called the sun once a year. Eight other planets also circle the sun. The planets and the sun make up our solar system. Our solar system is only one of billions of groups of stars and planets out in space.

Planets

A planet is a large ball of rock, metal, or gas that travels around a star, such as the sun. The planets near the sun, such as Mercury, are very hot. The planets far away from the sun, such as Saturn, are very cold.

Uranus travels around the sun between Neptune and Saturn. It is a cold planet with 15 moons and at least 11 thin, black rings.

Uranus

Earth

Earth is the only planet we know of where living things can survive. It has one rocky moon, which circles around Earth once every month.

Neptune is a cold, windy planet with eight moons.

Neptune

Pluto

Pluto is the planet farthest away from the sun. It would take the fastest spacecraft 10 years to fly from one to the other.

Saturn

Saturn has lots of rings around it. The rings are made of millions of pieces of rock and ice. Saturn also has at least eighteen moons.

Jupiter

Jupiter is the largest planet. It takes 12 years to go once around the sun.

new moon

The sun hardly lights up
the moon at all.

crescent moon

A quarter of the moon
is lit up by the sun.

full moon

The whole moon
is lit up by the sun.

The moon

Earth's moon has no light
of its own. It shines at
night only because light
from the sun shines on it
and we see this from Earth.
The whole moon is always
there but sometimes you
can see only part of it.

Mars   **Venus**

Mars looks red, so it is often
called the Red Planet.

Earth   **moon**

The sun

The sun is a very hot ball of glowing
gases. It gives off light and heat.
Without the sun, Earth would be
dark and cold, and there
would be no life. The sun
looks much bigger than
other stars because it is
much closer to us.

Venus is the brightest
object in the sky after
the sun and the moon.

Mercury

Mercury is the
closest planet to the
sun. It is boiling hot
by day and freezing
cold at night.

sun

Find out more

The Weather – page 42
Rocks and Soil – page 44
Light and Color – page 56

Traveling by Air

Find out more
Birds – page 30
Traveling on Land – page 50
Keeping in Touch – page 60

Flying is the fastest way to travel. People cannot fly like birds, but they can fly in machines such as hot-air balloons, airplanes, and helicopters. Astronauts even fly up into space in rockets and space shuttles.

Airplanes

The wings of an airplane do not flap up and down like a bird's wings. Their shape helps them to lift the plane up into the sky.

The wheels are used to land the plane and to move around on the ground.

The pilot moves flaps on the tail and wings to make the airplane turn and climb up or down in the air.

jet airplane

The pilot looks out of the cockpit windows at the front of the plane.

Space shuttles

A space shuttle is a spacecraft that blasts into space like a rocket. Then it glides back down to Earth using almost no power at all. A space shuttle can travel into space many times, carrying astronauts, experiments, and satellites.

take-off

flying through space

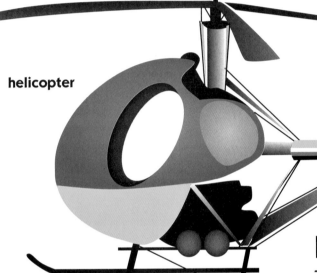

helicopter

Small rotor blades on the tail keep the helicopter from spinning in a circle.

Helicopters

The rotor blades on top of a helicopter spin around to lift a helicopter straight up into the air. The pilot changes the angle of the blades to move up or down, forward or backward.

The power of the jet engines pushes the airplane through the air.

Hot-air balloons

A small gas burner heats the air inside a hot-air balloon. This makes the balloon lighter than the cooler air around it, so it floats up into the sky. Lowering the flame in the burner lets the air in the balloon cool down, and the balloon sinks toward the ground.

Traveling on Land

Find out more
Jobs People Do – page 14
The Solar System – page 46
Traveling by Air – page 48
Traveling by Water – page 52

Most machines that travel on land have wheels that roll over the ground. Vehicles help people carry heavy things and travel long distances. Emergency vehicles, such as fire engines, help people in trouble.

Cars

The power to make a car go comes from its engine. The engine needs a fuel, such as gasoline, to make it work. Most car engines give off smelly smoke that makes the air dirty. Some car engines use electricity or the sun's energy for fuel, which are cleaner.

The steering wheel of a car turns the front wheels.

Trains

A train is a line of cars with wheels on the bottom that can carry many people, cars, or other heavy loads. A powerful engine pulls the train along narrow metal tracks attached to the ground.

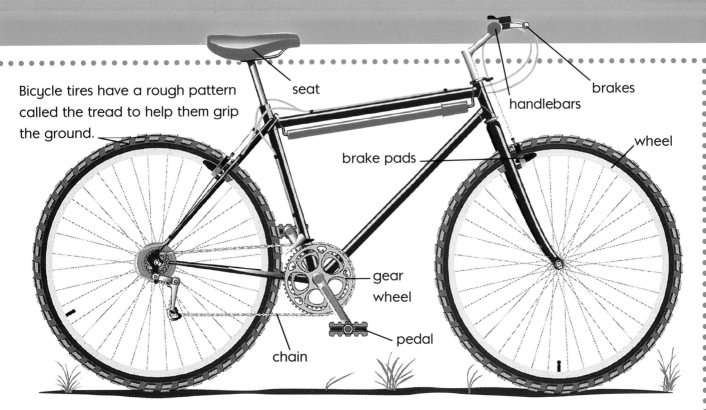

Bicycle tires have a rough pattern called the tread to help them grip the ground.

seat

brakes

handlebars

wheel

brake pads

gear wheel

pedal

chain

Bicycles

A bicycle has two wheels. When you push the pedals, the wheels turn. When you squeeze the brakes, the brake pads press against the wheels and make them stop turning.

Gears

The gear wheel has teeth around its outer edge. The teeth fit into other gear wheels or the holes in a chain. Gears change how much you need to pedal to make the bicycle go.

Traveling by Water

Small boats and large ships carry people and goods across water. The first boats were canoes and rafts. Next came sailing ships and then big metal ships with propellers turned by engines. Some modern cruise ships are so large they are like floating cities!

Find out more
Traveling by Air – page 48
Traveling on Land – page 50
Ice, Water, and Steam – page 55

Oil tankers

Huge ships called oil tankers have big tanks, or containers, for carrying oil. Some oil tankers can carry thousands of tons. They are so big that the crew ride bicycles around the deck!

Floating

A ship floats because it holds a lot of air inside its hollow shape. This makes it lighter than water. Underneath the ship, the water pushes up on the boat and keeps it floating on the surface.

Oars and sails

People use oars, paddles, and poles to push canoes, rafts, and rowboats through water. On sailboats, the sails catch the wind and pull the boats along.

The sails of modern sailboats are made of a strong fabric called nylon, which is made in factories.

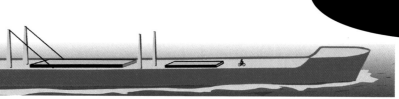

Propellers spin
around to push the
hovercraft along.

Hovercraft

Powerful fans on a hovercraft blow air under
the boat so it hovers, or hangs, above the
water on a cushion of air. A hovercraft can
go much faster than an ordinary boat
because it skims over the top of the waves.

The sails are attached
to the mast and the
deck with strong ropes.

Lighter cars
park on the top
levels of the ferry.
Heavy trucks go
on the bottom.

Ferries

A ferry travels back
and forth between
two places. It carries
people, vehicles,
and goods on short
trips over water.

The keel helps the boat
to balance and keeps it
from tipping over.

What Things Are Made Of

clay pot

Materials are the things that everything in the world is made from. Paper, wool, steel, gold, glass, and plastic are all kinds of materials. Materials can be bendy or stiff, rough or smooth, strong or weak, heavy or light.

Natural materials

Some materials do not have to be made in factories. Some, such as clay, oil, and gold, come from the ground. Others, such as wood, cotton, and wool, come from plants or animals.

newspapers ready for recycling

Recycling

Many materials, such as paper, steel, and glass, can be used over and over again. This is called recycling. It means we use less new material and throw away less trash.

plastic in-line skate

Artificial materials

Artificial materials, such as plastics, glass, steel, and cement, are made by people in factories. Glass is made from sand. Plastics are made from oil.

Find out more

Ice, Water, and Steam

Materials come in three different forms: solid, liquid, and gas. Water is an unusual material because it exists in all three forms in everyday life. It can be solid ice, liquid water, or an invisible gas called water vapor in the air.

Ice and water

iceberg

If liquid water gets very cold, it freezes into solid ice. Big chunks of ice floating in the sea are called icebergs. Ice floats because it is lighter than water. This is why ice cubes float in people's drinks.

Steam forms ———— when hot water vapor cools down into tiny drops of liquid water, which hang in the air.

steam engine

Steam power

In a steam engine, water is heated until it gets so hot that it turns into steam. The pushing power of the steam makes the wheels inside the engine turn. This gives the engine the power to move the train along the track.

Light and Color

The sun shines brightly to light your world during the day. At night, you can use electric lights. Light is made up of all the colors of the rainbow. Our eyes see different colors because of the way light bounces off of the objects around us.

the sun

Shadows

If something blocks out the light, a shadow forms behind it. A shadow is a dark area without light. Can you use your hands to make shadows that look like animals?

Reflections

When light hits a surface, it bounces back. This is called reflection. Flat, smooth, shiny surfaces like mirrors are the best at reflecting light. You can see your reflection clearly in a mirror.

raindrops

A rainbow has seven bands of color: red, orange, yellow, green, blue, dark blue (indigo), and violet. The colors always appear in the same order.

male peacock
showing off
its tail

Find out more

Amphibians – page 27
Birds – page 30
The Weather – page 42
The Solar System – page 46

Animal colors

The colors of animals help them to survive. A creature may have bright colors to warn other animals that it is poisonous to eat. Another animal may have colors that help it blend in with the objects around it. Birds like the male peacock use their colorful feathers to attract a mate.

Rainbows

When the sun shines through the rain, you sometimes see a rainbow in the sky. This is because the raindrops make the colors in the sunlight spread out so that you can see them.

Sound and Music

Find out more
Your Body – page 6
Jobs People Do – page 14
Amphibians – page 27
Traveling on Land – page 50

Sounds give you information. You make sounds by talking, singing, clapping, and whistling. Animals and objects such as musical instruments and doorbells also make sounds. Your two ears are specially shaped to collect sounds from all around you.

What are sounds?

When you throw a stone into a pond, water moves in ripples from where the stone hit the surface. Sound makes the air move in the same way. Sound is made up of waves that spread out in circles from the place it was made. You cannot see sounds, but you can sometimes feel them.

sounds from a radio

Hearing sounds

Sounds moving through the air travel right into your ears. There, they make your eardrums and ear bones shake very fast. This makes signals travel from your ears to your brain. Your brain figures out what the sounds mean.

Musical sounds

Guitars, drums, recorders, and pianos are all musical instruments. You can make musical sounds by twanging a string, banging a drum, blowing into a recorder, or pressing the keys of a piano.

The hole in the guitar makes the music louder.

guitar

Animal sounds

Animals use sounds for different things, such as attracting a mate, warning others of danger, or scaring an enemy. Some bats make high, squeaky sounds to help them catch insects in the dark.

Bats are the only mammals that can fly.

Some kinds of bats use their own squeaks to help them search for food and find their way in the dark. They listen carefully as sounds bounce off objects such as flying insects or walls.

A bat has large ears for hearing even very quiet sounds.

Keeping in Touch

Find out more
The Solar System – page 46
Sound and Music – page 58

It is easy to keep in touch with people all over the world by using telephones and computers. Telephones were invented more than one hundred years ago, but small computers that everyone can use have been around only since the 1980s.

Telephones

A telephone changes the sound of your voice into a signal that can travel a long way along wires or through the air. It also changes the signals it receives back into sound so you can hear people speaking.

Mobile phones

Mobile phones do not need wires. They use radio waves to send signals through the air to a series of towers. The radio towers pass on the signals until they reach the phone you are calling.

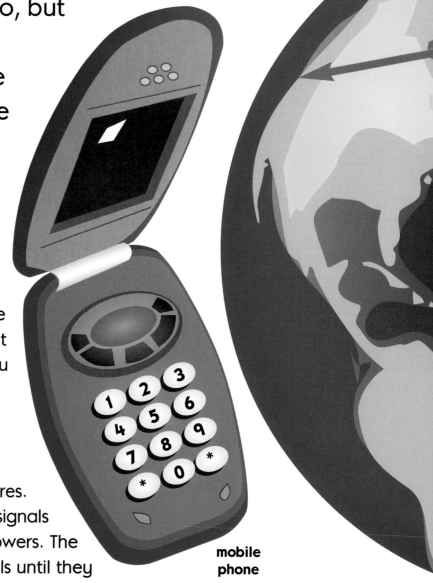

mobile phone

Satellites

Satellites out in space pick up signals from telephones in one part of the world and send the signals to another part of the world. This is much quicker than sending the signals across the surface of Earth.

The Internet

The Internet is a group of millions of computers all linked together. If your computer is linked to the Internet, you can get information, send messages, and buy things.

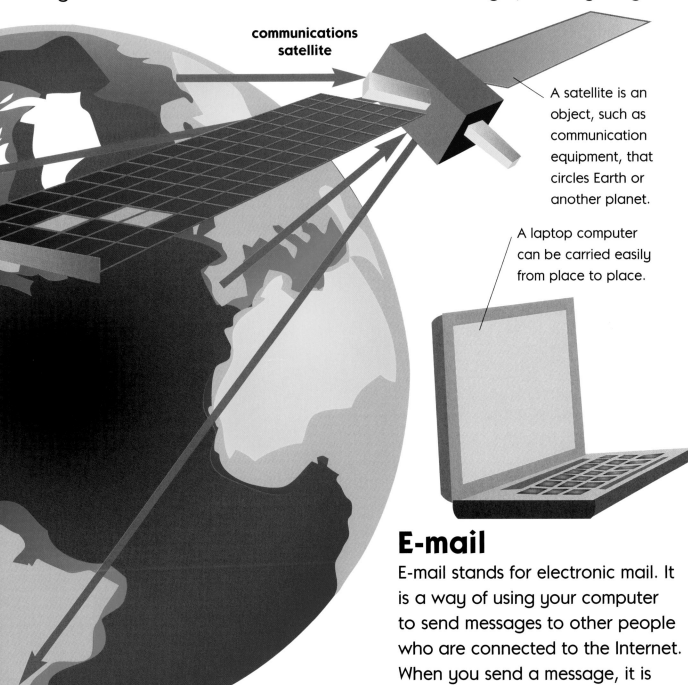

communications satellite

A satellite is an object, such as communication equipment, that circles Earth or another planet.

A laptop computer can be carried easily from place to place.

E-mail

E-mail stands for electronic mail. It is a way of using your computer to send messages to other people who are connected to the Internet. When you send a message, it is sent along the telephone network to another computer.

antennae long, thin stalks on an insect's head, which are used mainly for touching and smelling

astronaut a person who travels into space in a spacecraft

camouflage colors and patterns that blend in with the background. Camouflage helps animals hide.

carbohydrates foods that give you energy, such as rice and potatoes

conifer a tree, such as a pine, that makes its seeds inside cones. It has long, thin leaves that look like needles. The needles stay on the tree all year round.

coral a small sea animal that attaches itself to other coral on the ocean floor. Over time, their skeletons form reefs.

deciduous tree a tree, such as an oak, with wide, flat leaves. All the leaves fall off the tree in cold or dry seasons.

eardrum a piece of thin skin that stretches across the inner ear. It shakes when sound hits it. These movements turn into signals that travel to the brain.

e-mail electronic messages that you can write on your computer and send to people who are linked to the Internet

energy the power that makes things work or grow. Plants and animals get their energy from food. Machines get their energy from fuels such as gasoline.

fiber plant material that you eat to help food move easily through your body

fungus a plant-like object, such as a mushroom, that takes in food from plants and soil. It spreads by making spores.

gills small structures that animals such as fish use for breathing underwater. The flaps under the caps of mushrooms are also called gills.

Internet a communication system that links computers all around the world so that people can share information

lava hot, liquid rock that pours out of volcanoes onto the surface of Earth

materials the things that everything in the world is made from. Materials can be natural or artificial.

moon a ball of rock that travels around a planet. Earth has one moon.

petal part of a flower that is often large and colorful to attract insects and other animals to visit the flower. The animals take pollen from one flower to another.

pilot a person who flies an airplane

planet a large ball of rock, metal, or gas that travels around a star. Earth is a planet that goes around our star, the sun.

plankton tiny plants and animals that drift on water

pollen a dust made by flowers, which joins with plant eggs to make seeds for new plants

propeller a ring of large, curved blades that spin around to push a ship or aircraft forward or backward

radio waves signals that travel as invisible waves through the air, solid materials, and even outer space

rain forest a thick forest with tall trees, which is hot and wet all year round

recycling using materials more than once so that we do not waste them

reflection the bouncing back of light, heat, or sound from a surface

satellite a piece of equipment that circles a planet. Some satellites pick up and send information to and from Earth.

season a regular change in the weather throughout the year

seed a very young plant, wrapped in a protective case. With proper sun and rain, it may sprout into a full-sized plant.

senses the abilities of an animal to pick up information from the world around it. Hearing, touch, and taste are senses.

shadow a black shape formed when something blocks out light

skeleton a strong structure that supports and protects an animal's body

Solar System a group of planets and their moons going around and around a star, such as our sun

spore a small structure made by fungi and plants without flowers, such as ferns. Spores grow into new fungi or plants.

star a huge ball of gas in space, such as our sun. A star makes lots of light and heat.

tentacle a long, bendy part of the body that animals such as octopuses have near their mouths. Tentacles are used for moving, feeling, and holding.

tornado a whirling storm with very fast winds that travels over land

uniform matching clothes worn by people who do the same job or activity

vitamins substances in food that are needed to keep people healthy

volcano a crack in the surface of Earth through which boiling hot rocks, ash, and gases pour out. They form a mountain, which is also called a volcano.

water vapor an invisible form of water in the air. Liquid water becomes water vapor when it is heated. It is a gas.

wedding a ceremony that takes place when two people marry and promise to care for each other

Index